D0952514

Shakespeare
Bats
Cleanup

Koertge, Ronald.
Shakespeare bats
cleanup /
2003.
33305206237301
gi   07/30/04

Shakespeare
Bats
Cleanup

Ron Koertge

CANDLEWICK PRESS
CAMBRIDGE, MASSACHUSETTS

SANTA CLARA COUNTY LIBRARY

3 3305 20623 7301

This is a work of fiction. Names, characters, places, and
incidents are either the product of the author's
imagination or, if real, are used fictitiously.

Copyright © 2003 by Ron Koertge

All rights reserved. No part of this book may be
reproduced, transmitted, or stored in an information
retrieval system in any form or by any means, graphic,
electronic, or mechanical, including photocopying, taping,
and recording, without prior written permission
from the publisher.

First edition 2003

Library of Congress Cataloging-in-Publication Data

Koertge, Ronald.
Shakespeare bats cleanup / Ron Koertge. —1st ed.
p. cm.
Summary: When a fourteen-year-old baseball player
catches mononucleosis, he discovers that keeping a
journal and experimenting with poetry not only helps fill
the time, it also helps him deal with life, love, and loss.
ISBN 0-7636-2116-1
[1. Poetry—Fiction. 2. Baseball—Fiction.
3. Authorship—Fiction. 4. Diaries—Fiction.
5. Sick—Fiction.] I. Title.
PZ7.K81825 Sh   2003
[Fic]—dc21   2002031171

2 4 6 8 10 9 7 5 3

Printed in the United States of America

This book was typeset in Cheltenham.

Candlewick Press
2067 Massachusetts Avenue
Cambridge, Massachusetts 02140

visit us at www.candlewick.com

for bianca

Their pitcher walks our leadoff man. Greg moves him up to second with a perfect sacrifice. Fabian loops one into right.

I'm up. Two on, one out. I'm the cleanup man. My job is to bring these guys home.

I take a pitch. Foul one off. Take a strike. Their left fielder drifts in.

Bam! *I lift one right over his head. A double! Two runs score. I slide into second. Safe!*

That's what I'm thinking, anyway, propped up in bed with some dumb book.

Then Dad comes in and says, "The doctor called. Your tests came back. You've got mono."

"So I can't play ball."

He pats my knee. "You can't even go to school, Kevin. You need to take it real easy."

He hands me a journal, one of those marbly black-and-white ones he likes.

"You're gonna have a lot of time on your hands. Maybe you'll feel like writing something down."

In Bed

Being sick is like taking a trip, isn't it?
Going to another country, sort of.
A country nobody wants to visit.
A country named Fevertown.
Or Virusburg. Or Germ Corners.

The border guards are glum-looking,
with runny noses and pasty skin. Their
uniforms don't fit and flap open in the
back so you can see their big, ugly butts.

Nobody wants to go there, but everybody
does, sooner or later.

And some stay.

Pressure

Dad's never talked to me about writing before. He's not nuts to have me be just like him.

Len Boggs has a dad like that. It's been Boggs & Son ever since Lennie was about two seconds old.

They're plumbers. "Got clogs? Call Boggs!" Don't laugh. Their vans are all over the place. They're rich.

And Len hates it.

Lennie's fourteen, like me. He doesn't know what he wants to do when he grows up. Maybe go in the Marines. Maybe play the cello.

But he for sure doesn't want to be a plumber.

His dad is already on his case, riding him about it.

I think mine's just trying to be nice.

Home Alone

Well, not exactly. Dad's here, that's why
we don't have to get somebody to come
in and take care of me.

First of all, I don't need much care. I sleep
all the time, or at least it feels that way.

Dad works at home. He and I pass
each other in the hall—
I in my sweats, he in his cap.

When I was little and I got sick, Mom used
to read to me.

Thinking about that's not going to help.

Inquiring Minds Want to Know

Why am I writing down the middle
of the page?

It kind of looks like poetry, but no way
is it poetry. It's just stuff.

So I tiptoe into the den and cop this book
of Dad's.

It feels weird smuggling something about
poetry up to my room like it's the new
Penthouse.

But I don't want Dad to know what I'm
doing yet. Even though I'm not doing
anything. Not really.

I'm just going to fool around a little,
see what's what poetry-wise.

How Do You Do, Haiku

I thought I'd start small. I kind of
remember haiku from school last year.
I at least remember they're little.

But, man—I never saw so many frogs
in the moonlight. And leaves. Leaves
all over the place.

Weren't there any gardeners in ancient
Japan? Weren't there any cats and dogs?

Still, haiku look easy. Sort of. Five
syllables in the first line, seven
in the second, five in the third.

Frogs, frogs, frogs, frogs, frogs.
Frogs, frogs, frogs, frogs, frogs, frogs, frogs.
Frogs, frogs, frogs, frogs, leaves.

Very funny, Kevin.

At least I finished it. I can't finish anything
else, except my nap. Seventeen syllables
is just about right for somebody with my
reduced stamina. Perfect thing for an
invalid.

Oh, man — look at that: *in valid*. I never
saw that before.

    Just a single space
    in a word I thought I knew
    made the difference.

I Used to Be

a pretty good first baseman. I'm tall and
limber. With one foot on the bag, I can
really stretch. Somebody hits one right
back to the pitcher, he can just about
hand it to me.

For double plays, it's Walker/Jennings/
Boland. Short/second/first.

How many times did we practice that?
About a million.

Coach hits one to Walker, he flips
to Jennings, who burns one down to me.

Over and over so we don't think about it,
so it's automatic. No foot-on-the-bag,
eye-on-the-ball stuff. Thinking doesn't help.
Thinking gets in the way.

Man, a good double play is beautiful.
That's mostly what I miss, being part of
something beautiful. I know, I know. Guys
don't talk about stuff like that. But this is
between me and my journal.

See Ya Later

Lately I watch a lot of TV. I admit it.
I didn't used to, so my defense is that
mono made me do it.

My favorite show is *See Ya Later,*
the one where there's two guys and one
girl and the guys knock themselves out
trying to impress her because toward
the end of the show she has to say,
"See ya later," to one of them and the other
one she climbs all over and sticks
her tongue in his mouth. Right on camera.

I've probably watched a few too many
episodes, because I've been having these
dreams:

1. This surfer named Mike and I vie for
Gabriela. We meet on the beach. Mike
glides in on a surfboard. I lie down on
the nearest towel and take a vitamin.
She picks him.

(more)

2. A computer geek named Stan and I
meet Heather in a cyber-café. I'm hooked
up to an IV that drips the world's
strongest coffee right into a vein. Stan
shows Heather how to hack into her
school's computer and change all her
C's to A's. She picks him.

3. A paramecium and I meet Sandye
in a lab. He's in a petri dish; I'm asleep
on the table beside a Bunsen burner.
Sandye leans over the dish, then giggles.
She picks the paramecium because
she likes "a protozoan with a sense
of humor."

Monouglyosis

This can't be just plain mono. It's got to
be monouglyosis. I've got big circles
under my eyes, I'm skinnier than ever,
and I still have to wear my retainer.

There's a personal ad for you:

"Drab, emaciated teen with overbite
wants to meet pretty much anybody."

Dad brought home an *L.A. Weekly* the
other day and I was checking out those
personal ads in the back. Everybody wants
to take long walks on the beach.

What is that about? I'm surprised Pamela
Anderson can get to the water, there's
so many people walking hand in hand
in the sand.

For the Record

My name is Kevin Boland.

I live in Los Angeles (a suburb, actually).
I'm fourteen years old, I love baseball,
and I haven't got a girlfriend.

I'm just writing because I'm bored.
Thank God nobody's going to read it.

My dad's a real writer.

Picture this: There's a nuclear blast
or some humongous tidal wave.

Somebody in a HAZMAT suit finds
a novel of Dad's lying on a slightly
radioactive beach.

His big, fat, gloved fingers turn the pages.
He's got things to do, survivors to look
for, but he starts to read.

He's riveted. He can't put it down.

Gone in Sixty Seconds

I had a girlfriend a few months ago named
Sherry Toi.

This is an eighth-grade romance, okay?
Which means X tells Y she likes me. I tell
Y to tell X I like her, too. Then we start
sneaking looks at each other.

Y carries notes for us. Romeo and Juliet
we're not. No "Meet me at the crypt near
midnight. I'll be holding a torch. Beware
the white owl."

Y just shuttles these notes back and forth,
and eventually Sherry and I end up face to
face. I stand there staring at her lip gloss.

She's looking everywhere but at me, so
finally I blurt, "Why do you like me?"

Sherry frowns. She pouts while she thinks.
Her perfect forehead gets one little crease
while she searches for the answer.
Eventually she says, "Gee, I don't know."

And that's it. End of romance.

Confession

I liked Sherry Toi
because

she
liked
me
first.

In That Book of Dad's
I Borrowed

chapter two was about the sonnet.
Man, those made me want to go back to
haiku. Like a burger with everything on it,
sonnets are packed with roses and dew,
summer days, tender breaths, rocks and rills
(whatever rills are), and tons of wimpy guys
who apparently thought it was a thrill
to sit around with some sheep and sigh
about everything. I'm not that lame.
I'm just a former baseball whiz who'd like
to do what I used to do. Again.
Even if it means getting called out on strikes.
Sorry, Will, the sonnet's not for me.
Baseball's my love — not some thou or thee.

It Took Forever

to write that, and it isn't very good.
I finished, though, because I might be
skinny and sick but I'm not a quitter.

Man, sonnets are hard: counting
syllables in every line, trolling
for rhymes.

But it's really cool how everything fits
into fourteen little lines.

It's kind of like packing a lunch box,
getting in way more good stuff
than I thought I could.

When I E-mailed Greg

and said that I couldn't play ball for a
while, he came right over to the house.
Greg's a good guy, a good shortstop.

I staggered downstairs and sat
on the front steps. He stayed on his bike
like he's afraid he could catch this stuff
just being in the same hemisphere.

He leaned on his handlebars and said
not to worry. Bobby Carlyle could play
first base until I was better.

But he didn't look at me. Not really.
And he kind of talked at me. He did little
stationary wheelies, like his Huffy
was a wild stallion.

I Was Looking Out the Window

at the streets of Wellville, when I had
this thought: guys who drive convertibles
look like guys who ought to drive
convertibles.

If I had the money and if I was old enough,
I couldn't buy one. They wouldn't sell me
one. It'd be against some convertible law.

"Oh, no," they'd say. "Not with that
retainer. Not with that hair. We're sorry.
Come back when you're better-looking."

Remember Y?

That girl in my class who passed notes
back and forth for Sherry Toi and me?

Her name is Cassie Andrews, and she's
cute. She's got fast hair, short and slicked
back on the sides like she's standing
in a breeze.

When Greg came by, he said the word is
Cassie was thinking about liking me. But
not anymore, because I'm contagious.

Oh, who cares. When I get well, I'm going
to concentrate on baseball. Nothing
but baseball.

Since I'm in Bed So Much

I spend a lot of time in the past. "Reverie,"
my dad says.

I think about Mom, how she'd bring me
toast and juice and books. How she'd feel
my forehead and even (I was too old for
this but I liked it anyhow) kiss me
good night.

Dad worries about me, I know that.
But he's a guy. We're both guys:

"How ya doin'?"
"I'm okay."
"Don't overdo it."
"I won't."

It's not the same.

Why I Watch the History Channel

I used to follow the Dodgers and the Angels.
They're sort of local. Home teams.
But I watched everybody. I knew ERAs,
home runs this month, and who's on
the DL.

Not anymore. There's something
depressing about seeing guys do
what I can't.

Dad says it's just being sick and when I
get better I'll feel different.

Maybe. But what if I never get totally
better? What if I could never play
baseball again?

Then what?

Pizza with Nothing on It

Dad said I could meet Greg and Fabian
(he plays second base) down at Good
Knight Pizza if I took it really easy.

We used to go there after games all the
time, and Coach would spring for dinner.

I'm feeling a little better but — what's the
word? Oh, yeah — precarious. Like I could
feel worse again real easy.

The doctor wants me to stay away from
dairy products for a while — something
to do with my famous mega-sore throat.
So I scrape everything off my slice.

Man, do I feel like a major wuss.
Greg and Fabian suck up Cokes
and wolf down pizza with everything on it
but jelly.

I pick at my crust like a sick stork.

That Book I've Been Reading

is big on revision, which means, by
the way, not just doing something over
but seeing it again. That's kind of cool.

So I re-visioned that sonnet. I didn't
change much, but I did remember how
when I was looking for rhymes I was like
some guy pawing through his sock drawer
for a pair that matched.

But about halfway through, things started
to go smoother. I didn't have to try so
hard. The words kind of found me. I was
in the zone. Yeah, that's it.

Man, I've walked up to the plate knowing
I was going to get something I could hit. I've
shifted toward second because I just knew
that was where the ball was going to be.

That's the zone! Where you can do no
wrong. And I was in it again.

Just sitting at my desk.

Right After Christmas

I had a girlfriend named Rhoda Yu. She
was cool: she was cute, she was nice, she
made out when it was time to make out.

I got tired of her.

I don't like writing this down.
It makes me feel creepy and like some
kind of lowlife. But aren't you
supposed to be true to thine ownself?

I *had* to call her at 7:20.
We *had* to go out with at least one other
couple.
I *had* to eat lunch with her.
I *had* to carry her tray.
When I went up to bat, I *had* to look over
at her before every pitch.

The funny thing is when we did break up
she said, "It's because I'm Chinese,
isn't it?"

Under Construction

I'm kind of like a baseball diamond with
the grass mowed and the chalk lines laid
down, but there's no game.

Wait. That's not a very good simile.
Actually I'm more like a house that
was nice once and then had a fire
or something. Now it's being fixed up
from the inside out.

Yeah, that's better: my blood is getting
more nuclei, my spleen is shrinking,
my throat is like it used to be. But I am
not really involved. It's being done by
independent contractors.

Lengthy Reverie

When my buddies and I (eight of us,
counting our girlfriends) would go to
the movies at the mall, we had the most
fun when it was Dad's turn to drive.

Greg's father always had a couple
of drinks, Mark's acted like he was hauling
swine, and Fabian's mom asked us to look
for eligible men, if you can believe that.

Dad's Jeep is big, but we still had to put
a couple of kids all the way in the back
and squish everybody else together. Which
was great. And Dad played the radio loud,
even if it was an oldies station.

Inside the theater, we'd sit four in back/
four in front, so we could talk if we wanted
and pass junk food back and forth.

Waiting for Dad to pick us up after, we'd
all watch older guys in their own cars go
by with girls draped all over them.

Then in Dad's car the girls, our girls,
would do that a little, too. Practicing
to be sixteen.

Then we'd go to 13 Flavors. Dad always
bought stuff for everybody. We'd spread
out a little then. Maybe Rhoda and I'd go
upstairs with Fabian and Naomi or
outside by ourselves to watch the Gold
Line clatter past.

There's a nursing home a couple of blocks
away, and sometimes old people would
get wheeled down.

You know those rooms in the natural
history museum where Man goes from
this hulking hairball with bad posture
through a lot of different stages and he
ends up wearing green pants and holding
a golf club?

Well, 13 Flavors was kind of like that:
a new mom with a baby at one end,
an old lady in a wheelchair at the other,
and the rest of us somewhere in between.

Rhoda didn't like old people. Neither did
Greg. He said they smelled.

(more)

But my dad always ended up next to somebody really old, and he'd get them talking. It was actually kind of amazing: one minute there's this grandma type with pink, runny eyes kind of propped up by her attendant and the next she's got her hand on Dad's arm and her eyes are bright and she's telling him her life story.

He always says, "I'm a writer. I'm going to steal this." And they almost always say something back like, "Oh, good."

"'I'm a writer.'" That's a cool thing to say.

I don't mean I am, but I'm not a baseball player, either.

Not anymore.

Pantoum for Mom

She always used to sing
standing over the sink.
She'd splash water and suds,
after taking off her rings.

Standing over the sink
was her time to be alone,
after taking off her rings.
Dad and I upstairs or outside.

She needed time to be alone:
clients, husband, a boy like me.
Dad and I upstairs or outside,
she tuned the radio to 106.3.

Clients, husband. A boy like me
who used to tramp in mud.
She tuned the radio to 106.3.
Diagnosis? Dark, angry blood.

Who used to tramp in mud?
I did (but not on purpose).
Diagnosis? Dark, angry blood.
Months to live, then weeks, then days.

Just Not a Very Good Pantoum for Mom

Man, I almost cried writing that thing.
Poor little sick boy starts weeping.

You know what kept me from leaking
all over the page? Sticking to the rules
about what rhymes with what and how
two lines from one stanza turn into
two lines in the next.

It's funny. If I let myself go and wrote
about her getting sick, all I'd do is whine.
Instead, I made something semigood.

Mom would've liked it. Shoot, when I was
little I made this mug at YMCA camp,
and even I knew it looked like it came out
of a buffalo's behind and then he stepped
on it.

But it meant: *You're a great mom*.
She knew that. She even kept it out
where people could see it.

Well, nobody'll see this pantoum, but it
means the same thing: *You're a great mom*.

Were. You were a great mom.

Coach Mitchell

says to call him Mike but nobody does.
He played third for the St. Louis Cardinals.
Once. For a week or so, anyway.

Man, I'm impressed he was in the bigs
at all. Even for a minute.

Mr. Mitchell says a major-league
clubhouse is not to be believed: Jacuzzis,
whirlpools, clean uniforms your mom
doesn't have to wash, food just sitting
around all the time, and more towels
than anybody could ever use.

That's what he always mentions when
he tells us major-league stories. Those
towels. That and seeing a Cardinal
uniform hanging in his locker.

He got called up from triple A when
the Cards' regular third baseman pulled
a hamstring.

(more)

Coach couldn't believe big-league heat.
All he could do was stare. His scouting
report said, "Good glove, no bat."

I don't like thinking this, but I can't help it:
I hope Bobby Carlyle can't get around on
the fastball, either.

Weird Advice

A few months ago, we're having pizza
after we'd pulled one out in the last at bat
against the guys from Buttons 'n' Bows
(the fabric store that sponsors them).

Everybody's stoked. Mr. Mitchell downs
a couple of beers with his pizza, then
a couple more. The waitress is flirting
with him— that much is obvious.

He's a cool-looking guy with a mustache.
Still put together. Sure, she'd flirt.

Then her boyfriend comes in to pick her
up: he's in two-toned shoes and one
of those Hawaiian puka shell necklaces.

She gives Coach one more over-the-
shoulder glance and she's gone.

Mr. Mitchell slams his beer mug down.
I'm there, Greg, and a couple of other
guys. Everybody else is playing foosball
or Lara Croft: Tomb Raider.

(more)

"Stay away from women, boys," he says. "They'll end your career faster than a broken leg."

I just look down at my pizza. We all do.

Once some lady came to one of our games. She pulled up in a blue Miata, took a big cardboard box out of the back, and threw it onto the field. Turns out it's full of Coach's clothes and stuff.

We lost, 3–zip.

Another Mystery

Mr. Mitchell can't be the only grownup
with a secret life, I'll bet.

Mom was a travel agent. She went to
the movies (with Dad), read a lot,
played cards on Wednesday night.

That's all she did. At least it looked that way
to me. But what did I know? I was thinking
of myself all the time: my homework, my
girlfriend, my batting average.

But Mom wasn't just Mom. Her name was
Judy Simmons. She didn't want to be Judy
Boland or Judy Simmons-Boland.

She wanted to be Judy Simmons, like
she'd always been.

Was that the whole iceberg, or just the tip?

What about that time she came home
with a little tattoo on her ankle?

And Dad?

He could have a secret life, I guess. Or he
could have before I got mono, anyway.
Now I'm around.

I mean, I used to be at school. He was
home alone. Writing. Or doing . . .
whatever.

Dad used to teach high school. Now he
just writes, because my folks had these
huge life insurance policies.

They each got one from Mom's folks
in Florida for a wedding present. It was
a kind of family joke: right there with
the toasters and the blenders was this
cream-colored envelope with the policies
and the first ten years all paid up.

Dad always wanted to write full-time,
and now he gets to because Mom died.

At first he said he couldn't. He said he'd
never write another word and he'd grade
a million sophomore term papers all on
Silas Marner if he could just have her back
for one day.

After the Funeral

The neighbors came from all around,
   carrying casseroles.
They crept in the house without a sound.
   They buttered the toast and rolls.

They did this for a month at least,
   bringing us lunch and dinner.
But no matter how complete the feast,
   my father just got thinner.

All he could do was watch TV,
   the remote control in his hand.
He'd cry and wipe his eyes on his sleeve.
   He'd stare at the caravan

of junk that marched across the screen,
   watching for someone like Mom.
It might be a woman cleaning
   a stove, or waving a red pompom.

Then he'd sit up with eyes all wild.
   He'd listen to her voice.
He acted like a man beguiled,
   a man with no other choice.

(more)

This went on for weeks and weeks.
  No one knew what to do.
The stubble on his whiskered cheeks
  was like a grim tattoo.

The nights were long; he found no rest.
  He roamed both far and wide.
He beat his hands upon his breast.
  He missed his lovely bride.

Plain Words and Short Lines

That's what Dad's book said about
ballads, which also go *ba-dum-dee-dum,*
because they're a really old form, so
old that not everybody back then could
read and write but they could listen,
and the *ba-dum-dee-dum*s helped them
remember.

There's that old line about has-it-got-a-
beat-you-can-dance-to? Well, *ba-dum-dee-
dum* was the beat they could dance to.

That story in my ballad is pretty true, too.
People did bring lots of food. And Dad did
watch a lot of TV and cry, which freaked
me out.

I went back to school, but everybody kept
their distance, like if they got too close
maybe their mothers would die, too.

The Rules of the Game

School is over, and I did great. Passed
all my exams. Got good grades. Thanks
to Dad, who went by school and got my
assignments. And who was always just,
you know, there.

I was lying down the other day (big
surprise) thinking about poetry and
all those rules: rhyme this, repeat that,
count the syllables, look for stresses.

Man, I had enough rules before I was sick
(be home for dinner, wash your hands,
blah, blah, blah). And after mono it's no
running, no kissing, slow down, take it
easy. . . .

But then I had this thought: in baseball
it's nine guys on a side, four balls and
you walk, three strikes and you're out.

Those are the rules. Without them
there's no game.

Baseball and poetry aren't that different.

But Baseball and Sex?

Guys are always asking, "Did you get
to first base with her?"

So boys are the players and girls are,
what, the diamond?

What's weirder is that every guy talks like
he wants to hit a home run every time.

But I don't think he does. Not really.

And girls are for sure not supposed
to give up a homer easy. Second base
is sort of okay, but not third.

Dori Soretsky let Eric Oldham get to
second base. Now every guy who goes
with Dori expects to end up with a double.

Greg and Fabian were talking about how
they'd like to go with Dori.

Fabian said, "Maybe she wouldn't let
everybody. Maybe she just let Eric
because she liked him."

Greg said, "No, she'd let anybody now."

The Thicket of Indiscretion

When I was going with Goldie Overstreet,
just about all we did was meet at Draper
Park, sneak into the bamboo grove,
and make out.

We tried e-mailing but didn't have much
to say. She came to games, but she didn't
really like baseball.

We sat together for exactly half our lunch
period. Then she'd run over to her friends
and they'd look at me and giggle.

She ate weird: All her food had to be, like,
separate. No bean could touch another
bean, much less a carrot! If there was
gravy, forget it.

After a couple of weeks, I started to wait
for her to break up with me, because she
broke up with everybody. When she did,
I joined this kind of club: Goldie's Rejects.

And then we'd talk about her when she
wasn't around. And say crude stuff.

That's something I'm not too proud of.

More Poetry

It's afternoon. It's spring. We're standing
in bamboo. The air is heavy, damp, and green
(if air can have a color). Half-threatening
skies. We're kissing like there's no tomorrow.
I'm sweating. It's hotter than a greenhouse.
Kissing Goldie is making me crazy.
And the way she kisses back! Man, when I
was nine I thought that was the yuckiest
thing I ever heard. Now it's all I want.
I hoard these minutes in the green bamboo.
I jot them in the margins of the day
and look back when gloomy night by slow degrees
makes its way across my neighborhood.

That's Blank Verse

Weird name, huh? Sounds like it's written
in invisible ink. Actually, what makes it
blank is that it doesn't rhyme. But it's still
poetry because it's got to have ten (or so)
syllables in every line.

I mean, listen to this: Goldie and I used
to make out in the bamboo, and afterward
I'd think about it.

That's like journalism, right? Who did
what and where did they do it.

Poetry is richer, kind of, like chocolate
milk versus skim milk. They're both
nourishing, but chocolate milk
is just better.

I Never Wrote Poetry Before

Who came up with that line about
gloomy night making its way across
my neighborhood?

Not the Kevin Boland who was last
season's MVP. He didn't know a ballad
from a salad.

So it must be the Kevin who took off his
baseball uniform, put on some pajamas,
and picked up a pen?

Coach Mitchell Says

rules are there to be broken: feet shoulder-
width apart, knees slightly bent, blah blah blah.

Except some guys connect better with their feet
a little farther apart, or a lot closer together.

Poetry is that way: If the rules say five big
stresses per line, obviously four every now
and then isn't so monotonous.

If the rules say rhyme all the time, there are
these cool options called slant rhymes:
dog/dug, man/mean, tongue/lunge.
Stuff like that.

Like when you whisper something
to the person next to you and she
doesn't hear exactly what you said
but that turns out to be cooler, sometimes,
than what you actually meant.

Like that. Whisper-rhymes.

Yeah.

Haiku for Goldie

Greg and Mark came by. I'm almost
okay now. A lot better, anyway. For sure
not contagious.

They still treat me weird. Staying away.
No high-fives.

Here's the news: We beat Black & White
Cleaners and Pet Heaven. Sherry Toi's
going with some guy from Franklin.

Mark was nervous. He took a math book
out of his backpack, put it back, grabbed
a bottle of water, put it back, took out
a cardigan, put it back.

> I know we broke up,
> but what's that sweater doing
> in Mark's blue book bag?

No Candles/No Cake

Goldie turned fourteen when we were
going together.

Her parents are a drag. A major drag.
They both work downtown, they both
drive new Volvos, and they were in
Puerto Rico for her birthday.

I didn't want her to just get a present
from the UPS man and Grandma, so I
bought her a sweater from Out of the
Closet thrift store. It was a vintage
cardigan: white with a big purple
G on the chest. Breast. Whatever.

She really liked it. Made a big fuss.
Sort of cried.

Later, in the bamboo, she said she loved me.

Yoga Dad

That's right, every morning along with
this lady on channel 34.

He started a couple of months after Mom
died. I remember hearing this tinkly music
coming from his (it used to be their)
room, and when I glanced in he was
standing in his underwear crying.

Man, I didn't want to see that!

I've got to give him credit, though. He
stuck with it. Bought a pad with a tiger
on it. Got some loose pants.

Sometimes I catch him in these weird,
kind of pretzely poses, but he's pretty
good at it.

Dad's not a hunk. He's losing some hair
and he's got a big nose. But there are
a couple of neighbors who still bring
casseroles. Then they sit and have coffee.

I wonder if they think he's hot. Or do they
just want somebody nice to marry?
Because Dad's really nice.

And a Half-Order of Sestina, Please

One Halloween we all got dressed up.
I was Igor, Mom was the monster,
Dad was Victor Frankenstein. Instead
of just standing back with a flashlight,
my folks went trick-or-treating, too.
I've got a picture of us somewhere.

Next morning, when Mom had somewhere
to go, she put on her ghouly makeup,
got out her monster suit, and we drove to
the market. I held her big monster's
hand while she bought soap and light
bulbs. Other shoppers liked it. Instead

of moping around the store, instead
of just asking the manager where
they could find a twelve-pack of lite
beer, they grinned. Mom lit the place up.
It's funny what a random monster
will do. . . . .

Well, that's as far as I got on my sestina,
which is maybe the hardest form yet. Six
lines per stanza, six stanzas per poem,
and the same six words (but in a different
order every time!) at the end of every line.

It's like rub your stomach, pat your head,
whistle "Dixie," and don't think
of elephants.

I'm hard on myself when poems don't
work out, but I have to remember
that a guy who bats 300 (which is good),
screws up the other seven times.

Well, it was worth it to remember Mom
in her monster suit at Safeway.
Man, she was fun.

SUV Dad

It was an impulse about six months ago.
He just drove onto the lot in one car and
drove off in a black Jeep.

He says he knows it's silly and it does
guzzle gas a little and he'll probably never
use the four-wheel drive.

We catch Jeep ads on TV: guys who need
a shave fording raging rivers or prowling
the African veldt on a photo shoot.

And Dad? He goes to Staples for reams
of computer paper or Kinko's to get his
stories copied.

I guess he just didn't want to be
somebody who drove a white Camry
with a reputation for reliability.

That guy's wife died.

Twelve Couplets = One Poem

I've got Barry Bonds hanging on the wall
big as life. He gets more wood on the ball
than anybody. It doesn't take Sherlock
to figure out that this is a jock's
room: a dozen Rawlings baseballs, a bat,
a glove = paraphernalia of combat.
A nervous pitcher fights to keep control,
the fastest runner (already he's stolen
one) dances down the line like a mad gnome,
the catcher hunkers down, protecting home.
That's the way it used to be: I'd just lope
up to the plate, I'd hit a frozen rope
toward some poor shortstop with an iron glove.
He'd blink. My batting average would improve.
Now I dream of sitting in the doctor's cool
white room. Diplomas from a dozen schools
hold up the walls. He comes in, seems cheerful.
Dad scoots forward in his chair. I'm fearful.
The doctor flips through tests one by one.
He folds them up, their usefulness all done.
"You're fine," he says, "just a little gaunt.
Get out of here and find a restaurant.
Celebrate this long-awaited day.
Take it easy, but go on and play!"

See Ya!

For the record — that last poem was in
couplets, which are (obviously) a couple
of lines that rhyme and walk that old
Shakespeare walk (which is called iambic
pentameter).

It really isn't that good a poem. It's kind of
in pieces, and I had to hammer in some
of those rhymes just to make them fit.
Maybe I got a minor-league muse?

Not that it matters. I probably won't write
any more poetry. I probably won't even
write in this journal thing anymore.

It's kind of girly. And, anyway, I'm back
in the game!

Well, Maybe Just One More

I called Greg and told him I was out of jail.
He wasn't as stoked as I thought he would
be. As I wanted him to be.

He even said, "Carlyle's pretty good."

Man, stick the knife in and twist it,
why don't you?

Make the noose a little tighter.

Give me two kinds of poison.

Use all six bullets.

Formal Retraction

I said I wouldn't write anymore,
but I take that back.

When I got sick, I missed baseball.
When I got well, I missed writing.

Amazing.

Good News

Coach said I'm not in shape but I could
still dress for the game on Saturday
with Gus's Barbecue.

All right!

Mom's Car

I washed my uniform for Saturday because
it had been folded up for weeks, and I
wanted to look good even if I wasn't
going to play.

The laundry room's right next to the
garage, so I couldn't help but see it: Mom's
Buick with 32K miles on the odometer.

Dad says it's mine when I'm sixteen.
I don't know.

Right after she died, I'd go out there
sometimes and just sit in it.

It smelled like her. There was this Kleenex
wadded up in the ashtray. A pen she liked.

I'd put my hands on the wheel where hers
had been. Turn on the radio and listen
to her stations.

Look in the rearview mirror that might
remember her eyes.

Life in the Country

Somebody gets good wood on the ball.
The shortstop spits affectionately
into his glove. Uniforms are polar
white, cleats clean as teeth.

The stands rumble and hum.
Somebody's burgers sizzle on
the grill. A catcher shambles
toward the plate. The trees

seem extra green. Girls I know
preen at the water fountain.
A baby touches its own nose
as someone strokes a single
and doesn't try for two.

He stands on the bag, tugging
at his batting glove and watching
the umpire dust off home plate
like a maid.

The Pastoral

is a kind of poem that doesn't have
rules about rhyme or meter, but it's
always about how nice it is not to be in
the city. And that's because the Industrial
Revolution made things all smoggy and
smoky and people who worked in
factories kind of felt like slaves.

So they liked to read about shepherds
and drinking fresh water out of streams
and living in the country.

"Life in the Country" is about how much
I like being back in the dugout, how green
and peaceful a ball field is, how easygoing
a baseball game can be.

I'm Riding the Pine

which means sitting on the bench
which means not playing.
So I'm revising "Life in the Country."

I'm still trying to slip in some inside
rhyme, just a few things that chime
a little but don't go *bong, bong, bong*
at the end of every line.

So when Bobby Chu gets a hit (he's
the one tugging at his batting glove),
I don't stand up and yell like the others,
because I'm working on my pastoral.

Shoot, I'm on the bench. At the end.
I'm not going to play.

But Coach storms down and reams me:
"Boland! At least act like you're part
of the team."

The other guys look at each other. I stand
up, but it's too late. They're all sitting
down now.

I put the poem away.

We Win

No thanks to me. But I get in line, anyway,
and do that halfhearted handshake with
Gus's Barbecue.

But when we all huddle up and do that
"One. Two. Three. Team!" thing, I'm
on the outside looking in.

My hand's not on Coach's or Greg's
or Mark's.

I'm back with Ernesto, Lloyd, Rafael,
and Akim, guys who always ride the pine,

guys who never get to play unless we're
up 10–zip and it's the bottom of the sixth.

I remember not even watching, just
hearing the ump call them out on strikes.

Now I am them.

I Hear Myself

tell Greg and the guys I'll skip the pizza,
thanks. I'm a little tired.

It's true and it's not true. Mostly I'm
embarrassed. I'm not used to feeling
out of it.

And I don't want to sit at the wrong end
of the table with the losers.

And then I'm embarrassed at that because
it's not nice. Mom hated it when I wasn't
nice.

I'm thinking all this while parents are
picking kids up and guys are getting their
stuff together. Goldie is sizing up Bobby
Chu (he went three for four and drove in
the last two runs). It looks like Chu will
get a turn in the bamboo.

Also Goldie is introducing this new girl,
Mira Somebody, who just moved here.
She's real tall with one long braid down
her back outside some floppy overalls.

(more)

She's holding a book instead of a cell phone, and you don't see that very often!

Then everybody splits. For home. Or for pizza. Mira and I wander off in the same direction. Then out of nowhere she says, "What were you writing?"

Huh?

"You were writing something while everybody else was playing or watching."

"No, I wasn't."

Well, That Was Stupid

So I want to run after her and explain. Say
I lied but it wasn't a big lie, just a dumb one.

But her mom's waiting for her, standing
by an Acura. With her arm out. So Mira
has a place to go.

My mom used to do that, but not at the
ball field. At home, with nobody around
but me and Dad. In the kitchen mostly.

I'd come in from school or from practice.
Mom would hold out one arm and I'd walk
right into it. Under it, sort of.

I liked to put my forehead against her
collarbone.

Ollie, Ollie, All in Free

It's okay to come out now, Mom.
I've looked everywhere. In the closets,
downstairs, in the garage, the attic.

I know you've found a really cool place
to hide, but it's been long enough now,
okay?

Come out, come out, wherever you are.

It's dark, and you're really late for dinner.

Contemporary Elegy

"Ollie, Ollie, All in Free" is an elegy,
which is, my book says, any lament.

In the old ones, there are lots of bedewed
cheeks and sorrow with a capital *S*. Plus
brown leaves, almost for sure an urn,
and about ninety-nine pounds of dust.

Mine's a modern one. It's got a garage in it.

It's still sad, though.

I wonder if I'm thinking about Mom more
because I lost my place in the starting
lineup.

Did losing that little thing make me
remember losing something big, like one
little match can start a whole forest fire?

Cruising

The next day, I ride my bike past Mira's
house, which is right by Goldie's. I'm
hoping Mira will be outside, but she isn't.

So I ride past the other way.
And back again.
Then forth. And back.

This time she comes out, down the walk,
and right to the curb. She's wearing a
yellow top, blue pants, and sandals.

"What are you doing?" she asks.

I stay on my bike, but take off my cap.

"You know when you asked me if I was
writing something and I said I wasn't?
Well, I was."

She puts both hands in her pockets. Her
hair isn't in a braid anymore. It's loose,
and there's tons of it.

"So what were you writing?"

"It doesn't matter. But I felt funny about telling you I wasn't writing something when I was."

"Were you keeping score?"

"No."

"Were you writing a letter?"

"No."

"A poem, maybe? You don't look like those other guys. You look sensitive."

"Are you kidding? No way am I sensitive. I gotta go."

Another Smooth Move

Well, wasn't that wonderful!

I ride over there to say
I told a little lie

and I end up telling
another one.

Try, Try Again

There's no Acura in the driveway this
time but there is a Ford Taurus.

I circle in front of her house. I like feeling
my legs work. I got out of shape fast.

Finally I decide to just knock on the door.
Which is bigger than the door to my
house. More ornate. There's even this
huge horseshoe-shaped knocker. But
when I raise it, a doorbell inside goes
bing-bong.

Too weird.

I hear footsteps. Heavy ones. Either Mira
has gained a hundred pounds overnight
or she's got a big brother, and I mean big.

"Yes?"

Oh, man. It's her dad. Mr. White-Shirt-
and-Tie, for God's sake. And me in some
thrashed shorts.

"Uh, is Mira home?"

(more)

He looks at me suspiciously. He squints.
He frowns. *"Un momento."*

While he's gone, I check out the foyer:
red tile floor, a little fountain thing
against one wall, big mirror over that.
Golf clubs leaning in the corner.

When Mira glides toward me, I blurt,
"It was a poem. But I'm not sensitive.
I'm a ballplayer. I was just fooling around
with poetry when I was sick with mono."

"So you lied."

"Just a little one."

She's got all her hair in that braid again,
and she's playing with it. She holds the
end like a microphone: "Thomas Jefferson
said, 'He who permits himself to tell a lie
finds it much easier to do it a second and
a third time.'"

"How did you know that?"

"I had to write a book report. But I just remember things. Don't you?"

"Most home runs by a first baseman, maybe. Not things Thomas Jefferson said."

"Are you any good?"

"At baseball?"

"At poetry."

"No. I don't know."

"You should show me something."

"A double play, maybe?"

"That you wrote."

"I don't think so."

"Mira! *Venga, por favor.*"

She half turns. She's got a killer profile.

(more)

"Okay, Dad, I'll be right there." Then real soft: "I'm glad you came by, Kevin. You can e-mail if you want, but I'm never going into the bamboo with you like Goldie."

"How did you know about that?"

"What do you think girls talk about — poetry?"

So I Won't Forget

I smoke home chanting her e-mail
address. Well, I smoke for a few blocks
then slow down because I get spaghetti-
leg pretty easy.

Dad's Jeep is in the driveway. He's
probably writing. I make a protein drink,
take my B complex vitamin, go upstairs,
and log on.

Her address is easy to remember:
Miramira@micasa.com. So I start with that:

"I like your user name. As in Snow White,
right? When the Wicked Queen asks who's
the fairest. (Actually, *wall/all* isn't that
original a rhyme.)"

I clean up my room then. Put some whites
in a pile, add a couple of shirts to the go-
to-cleaners bag. Then the iMac says I've
got mail!

"Are you sure you're not a poet, Kevin?
Or do you just point out uninspired
rhymes to all the girls?"

(more)

I shoot right back: "I'm just a first baseman, ma'am."

Immediately: "Before I forget— my dad can't know we're e-mail friends, okay? He thinks every boy is part of a mutant army that rules the night and doesn't think of anything except innocent young girls."

"Is there anything I could do to make him like me?"

"Sure. Move to Paraguay and become a priest."

"I'll have to ask my dad."

"What's Up?"

It's Dad on his way down the hall, a pencil clutched between his teeth.

I say, "Not much." He says, "Want to play some catch?"

Dad's not much of an athlete. Sometimes he throws underhand. But this is for me. I know that, and it's nice of him to do it.

We stand maybe twenty yards apart. I like using my body again. I know it's going to take a lot of practice before things come natural. Weird, huh? All that work to act natural.

I have to admit that while this re-education is going on (I picture my cells, all at their little desks, their *Basics of Baseball* texts in front of them), I'm thinking about Mira, too. How she said "uninspired rhymes."

That was right on the money.

I Work Out with the Team

Oh, baseball, I've missed you. You don't
care if I'm skinny and get out of breath
easy. You have wide arms. You can take
everybody in, the (1) ept and the (2) inept.
And even the (2)'s have fun, which I know
is true because I'm a (2) now — taking
those whiffy swings, getting thrown out
by a mile, sitting down at the wrong end
of the bench with the other (2)'s, who
turn out to be good guys.

So I'm not the Kevin I used to be. I'm just
glad to be back — my heart beating
baseball, my nose sniffing baseball.

No more ghosting around my own house.
No more living secondhand. No more
postponing things. Just standing in my
cleats again, a clean uniform on my
unremarkable arms and legs, all of me
just ecstatic to be out there under the
invisible stars, playing baseball again.

The Land of the Free

Free verse in this case. Because that's
"I Work Out with the Team."

That book of my dad's says how American
free verse is. How democratic. That just
like the Pilgrims came over here to be free,
somewhere along the line poets wanted
to be free, too. They didn't want to rhyme.
They didn't want to count syllables.

Makes sense to me. "I Work Out with the
Team" really was easier to write without
all those rules.

I gotta say, though, that the poems before
the free verse one were better in a way.

So is that what Mira's parents are
thinking? That if they go by the rules,
their daughter will be better?

Poetry, Poetry Everywhere

A couple of days later, Dad says to me, "There's this poet I like a lot, and he's reading in Venice Wednesday night. Do you want to go? I won't tell your friends. We'll wear disguises if you want."

"Can I bring somebody?"

"I thought you were through with girls."

"This one's pretty interesting."

"If you say so."

"You're going to have to call her parents. Or I can move to Paraguay and become a priest."

Dad just looks at me.

Weather Report: E-Mail Flurries, with Slight Accumulation

Mira
Since it's a poetry reading, we could say
that it's educational.

Me
Absolutely. A cultural experience.
Expansive in every way.

Mira
We'd have to be back by ten.

Me
Even if we have to leave in the middle
of an ode.

Scrutiny

On the day of the reading, I wash the Jeep.
After dinner, I put on khakis and a white
shirt. Dad comes downstairs in shorts
and Pumas. I ask him to change. On the way
to Mira's he says, "Now *I'm* nervous."

I write haiku in my head, counting
seventeen syllables on my knee
but around the crease in my new pants.

As we trudge up the walk, I kind of wish
I was in Japan. With a frog and a leaf.

Mr. Hidalgo invites us in. Everything
shines — fingernails, shoes, floor.

His wife stands beside him, also very
shiny. She's got on high heels and a dress
with lots of buttons.

Jeez. This is their idea of relaxing after
dinner?

When Mira comes down, her father
inspects her. I'm kind of waiting for
someone to salute.

Mr. Hidalgo asks, "Do you have a cell, Mr. Boland?"

Dad shakes his head.

"Mira can take mine. Just in case."

Dad steps off the porch first. I shake hands with Mira's parents again.

Her dad's smile might be made of iron.

On the Road (Plus One Couplet)

Mira and I sit in back. Dad drives.
We take the Pasadena Freeway, oldest
in L.A. It winds like none of the others,
and Mira leans into me, then doesn't
unlean.

Dad reaches for the radio. On comes
Vin Scully, voice of the Dodgers.
But not too loud.

She asks about the game and tilts
her head to hear my dad better. Her hair
is gorgeous against her white sweater.

Everything she does, she does with ease
away from her parents' tyrannies.

Venice (California)

The reading is in a bookstore right beside
a bar. Inside there's a semicircle of chairs.
Mira and I are almost the only kids.

We're barely inside when her phone rings.
A few people scowl at her. She doesn't
even say hello. "Thank God you called,
Dad. Kevin's father got lost and drove
right into the ocean, which is lucky in a
way because we were on fire. Can you
come and get me? Better hurry.
The sharks are closing in. Bye."

"Isn't he going to be mad?"

"Do you know the word *ambivalent*?"

"Uh-huh."

"My dad's ambivalent about me."

"So he's going to be half-mad?"

"Something like that."

Afterwards

We're standing outside while Dad talks to the writer he came to see.

I ask, "Which was your favorite poem?"

"That's easy. 'Here Comes the Blues in Corrective Shoes.'"

"Me too. But I liked it when that girl who read first rhymed *catharsis/the farce is*."

"She was pretty."

"Not as pretty as you."

She rolls her eyes, "Is that something your teammates told you to say?"

¡Arriba!

When we get back in the car, Mira reaches
for her seat belt. "This is my mom's idea
of poetry." And then she recites

> *Para mirar tu sonrisa*
> *tengo mis ojos;*
> *Para ver mi alegría*
> *tengo espejos;*
> *Para alimentarme,*
> *tengo maíz y arroz —*
> *Para ponerme a cantar,*
> *amor, eres mi voz.*

I look at her as seriously as I can:
"Did Thomas Jefferson write that, too?"

Mira laughs as Dad translates,

"Something about gazing and eating corn
and rice. And the last two lines are,
'To break into song, love, you are my
voice.' Right?"

(more)

Mira applauds. "Very good. Mom says
Dad used to whisper it to her."

I think about that most of the way home:
her dad not in a suit, but jeans, maybe,
and a T-shirt. Whispering poetry to girls.

At Her House

my dad waits in the car. Hers opens the
door and stands there until Mrs. Hidalgo
comes and drags him away.

Mira and I walk slowly. Really slowly.
Finally, we climb the steps. She stands
on the last one so she's taller than me.
She leans in. "Your hair smells good."

"I'll bet yours does, too."

"Let's see." She drags about a bushel of it
over her shoulder. Just then, the porch
light goes off, on, off again.

Mira sighs. "My father has my hair
booby-trapped. Anytime a boy puts
his nose in it, no matter where I am,
the lights flicker."

After Practice

Greg, Mark, and Fabian slither over.

"Too bad we don't play night games,
Boland. All that moonlight in June
would be right up your alley."

"You gonna trade your cap for a beret?"

"You're not too sensitive to bat, are you,
Shakespeare?"

I pound my glove.

Hotmail

Me
How'd they find out?

Mira
I told my girlfriend. I guess she told
somebody.

Me
Mira, that was a secret!

Mira
Why? It's cool that you write poems.

Me
Tell that to Greg and Mark and Fabian.
They're probably going to get me a pink
jockstrap.

Mira
What about Octavio Paz?

Me
Who?

(more)

Mira
Only Mexico's greatest poet.

Me
Oh, yeah? Well, what's Octavio's batting average?

Mira
Are we fighting, or is this just a squabble? It doesn't feel like a fracas, but it might be a small fray. Skirmish, maybe?

Me
Man, you really know a lot of English.

Mira
Kevin. I was born in Minneapolis.

The Surprise

I come in from jogging and Dad stops me
in the hall.

"Your girlfriend's father called."

"It wasn't 'Pistols at dawn' or anything
like that, was it?"

Dad grins. "He was very polite. Very."

"Did you know Mira was born
in Minnesota?"

"Actually, yes. Her father and I talked
for a few minutes. He was a hospital
administrator there just like he is here."

"So what did he call about?"

"He wants to know if we'll come to a party
this Saturday. For his mother-in-law."

"Both of us?"

"Uh-huh. I told him I'd check with you."

(more)

"Sure. Yeah. Do you want to?"

"Why not? I'll practice my Spanish. Mom'd like that." He rubs his forehead. "It's funny. I'm not forgetting her, but I don't think about her all the time anymore."

"I know. And it makes me feel weird."

He reaches. Pats me. Hard. "Me, too."

Then that's over.

"Want to go out?" he asks. "Or I can cook something and we'll stay home."

"Let's stay home."

En Casa

I guess Mira's got a lot of relatives —
cousins and stuff — that she hangs with.
Greg sent me an e-mail that somebody
forwarded to him about how the girls
we know don't like going to Mira's
because her mom is always around.

Mark's mom (single) is on call at the hospital
24/7. Or at least it seems that way.

Greg's is forever flying someplace
or other on business.

Goldie's mom is never home.

Dad always wants to know where I am.
I have to be home for dinner. If I'm
going to be late, I have to call.

My friends think that's stupid.

I don't, but I'm not going to tell them that.

About Saturday

Mira says to dress casual. We'll be
eating in the backyard. There'll be a piñata
for the little kids, maybe softball.

I lay out my clothes. My shorts
and T-shirts. What goes with what.

When I was little, my folks took me to
the arboretum so I could feed the ducks.

They have these peacocks out there.
They'd run at me and try to get the bread
I was carrying for Donald and Daisy Duck.

Once the peacocks had robbed me, they'd
open up their big tails and strut around,
showing off for the girls.

My T-shirts are all different colors.
I fan them out. I scrutinize
the available plumage.

Secret Couplets

Dad puts the directions in my lap.
I feel like somebody in an Aesop
fable, making his way to the treasure
(but in this fable there's a chauffeur).
We pass a yellow house, then a blue one.
The air is great. It smells like cinnamon.
A man yawns and rubs his shaved head.
He waves at a friend carrying bread
and *leche.* The streets are full, porches, too.
It makes my neighborhood seem subdued.
I like these busy little restaurants.
I like that lady's matching dogs that pant
and beg for treats. Nobody has a dog
where we live. Everybody seems to jog
alone with their earphones. Retirees
close the blinds and watch their huge TVs.

"You okay?" Dad asks. "What are you
doing?"

"Uh, just writing something down.
Something for school."

"Are you kidding? It's June."

(more)

97

I can't tell him I'm writing couplets. Weird,
huh? The guys know. Now anyway. Thanks
to Mira.

But if I told Dad, he'd want to see.
And then he'd feel like he had to say
something encouraging.

To Grandma's House We Go

It turns out to be a pretty nice one
in a not-so-nice part of town.

The big porch is made out of rocks
(fieldstones, Dad says). The whole place
is kind of low-looking with neat brown
shingles (California-bungalow style,
Dad says).

A couple of kids about as old as me are
painting over some tagger's personal ID.
They've got a tarp down so nothing gets
on the sidewalk.

I spot Mira just as she spots me. I like
how she runs toward us. She kisses my dad
on the cheek, puts her arm through mine.

We make our way inside. There are a lot
of books. Big picture of Jesus (He's always
so serious). Something smells really good.

In the kitchen Mr. and Mrs. Hidalgo stand
up and shake hands. He's in slacks and a
loose shirt: Mr. Casual. But he's spotless.
Perfect.

(more)

Mira's grandma eyes me. "Ah," she says. "The *novio*."

Mira's dad scowls.

Outside

I ask, "What's a *novio*?"
"Boyfriend. She likes to tease my dad."

"He doesn't seem like the kind of guy who
gets teased much."

"Tell me about it."

We stroll around. A few sixteen-year-old
girls sit together. It seems like they're
wearing all the makeup they own. When
Mira introduces me, they don't even look
up. We're boring. Everything's boring.

Out by the street, some guys lean on this
tricked-out Malibu. I shake hands with
a cop, an architect, an artist. They speak
English, then Spanish, then both in the
same sentence. I get some of it, and smile
at the right places. I hope.

We're watching those kids finish up
painting over the graffiti. Mira's got her
arm around my waist.

(more)

"Dad pays them," she says. "Every week. If they get good grades, he pays them extra."

At Least One *Muy* Weird Thought

While Mira goes to get Cokes, I sit in
a big wooden chair whiter than I am.
There are speakers in the trees and some
CDs playing. I pick out words that Mom
taught me.

I start thinking that if I took Spanish all
through high school and all through
college, by the time I got out
I'd be pretty good at it.

A lot of ballplayers are from the
Dominican Republic and other places
where everybody speaks Spanish. How
cool would it be to talk to those guys!

And I could translate stuff, too. Not just
for the other players, but . . .

Wait a minute. Am I actually fantasizing
about winning the game with a long
double in the bottom of the ninth
then sitting in my room translating
Octavio Whateverhisnameis?

Park/Ark

I'm sitting by myself wishing I had some
paper and a pen when this lady sits down
beside me. "You okay?"

I nod. "I think so."

"I just told your dad: Don't try to keep
everybody straight. It'll make you crazy.
They'll sort themselves out." She points to
one of those guys I shook hands with, the
cop, I think. "Bobby and I got married two
years ago. I still get Aunt Somebody mixed
up with Tía Somebodyelse."

Just then a little boy toddles up to us.
He's holding a can of ginger ale. "Mama,"
he says, "*por favor.*" He's as blond as she is.

When she leaves, I go back to thinking:
maybe park/ark is too easy. Park/stark?
Nah, too bleak. Park/pork? Oh, that's great:
"Noah, bring the pigs on next!"

"Hey, *flaco!*"

Flaco I know. *Flaco* means skinny.

I look up. Some guy is standing over me
with a mop handle. Even his shadow
is heavy.

"Word is you're the ballplayer." He points
to a piñata hanging from a rope. "Think you
can hit that?"

Mira hustles over. "Roldolfo, leave him
alone!"

He leans over me, right into me. He hisses,
"You're, what, fourteen? You want to live
to be fifteen, you keep your hands off my
cousin!"

Batter Up

I take the mop handle, glance up at the
piñata. Which is this little bull or horse,
usually, made out of paper mache,
and filled with candy.

It's hanging from a rope and somebody at
the other end either lets it down or pulls it up.
A kid with a stick is blindfolded. When
he hits it hard enough, candy flies out.

Roldolfo grabs the bat. "I'll show you how
to do it." A girl ties the handkerchief.
His pals parade around, showing off
their muscles.

Mira whispers, "He thinks he's so tough."

"Well that makes two of us, because I think
he's so tough."

Mr. Hidalgo frowns as Roldolfo steps up.
People stop to watch.

He swings and misses. He swings again.
And misses. Once more. This time so hard
he falls down. A few people laugh.

He says something in Spanish, something
bad, because all the moms shake their
heads and hustle the little ones away.

He tosses me the bat. "Your turn, big shot."

Mira takes the blindfold, turns me around,
whispers while she ties it. "Go bravely
into battle, Sir Flaco. They will sing about
this around the campfires forever."

"I'm glad you think this is funny, Mira."

Roldolfo's crew is calling me names
I'm glad I can't understand.

Thank God I've got a plan: I'll listen
for the hiss the rope makes, then swing
where I'm pretty sure the piñata isn't.

(more)

I plant both feet and uncork one.
Everybody groans. I guess I was closer
than I thought!

Then the guy starts jiggling it; I can hear
the candy inside. This time I swing from
the heels, miss for sure, and go down
on one knee.

Half a fall. That should satisfy old Roldolfo.

Mira whips off my blindfold, kisses me on
the cheek. Everybody applauds. I bow like
a big ham.

7:30 P.M.

The fire writhes and snaps.
A woman in a blue smock
pets two ancient cats.
Someone glances at a clock.
Mira puts one hand on my heart.
Like passengers, people disembark.

Cars go by in a blur.
A girl sits on the porch,
a boy kneels beside her
like an idolater.
The kids are too tired to play.
This is the end of the holiday.

On the Way Home

I write "7:30 P.M." in the car, and it's just
an okay first draft except for the line
about the idolater.

I really like how words that I know but
never use just show up. (How often do I
say *idolater* in the dugout?) Like they've
been in the on-deck circle just about
forever, patiently waiting.

In the bigs there's the DH, the designated
hitter. Maybe in poetry, there's a DW,
the designated word?

Almost Home

Dad says, "That was a nice thing you did."

"What thing is that?"

"C'mon. I've seen you bat a thousand
times. You never swing from the heels.
If you'd hit that piñata, the kid who was
hassling you would've been madder.
Maybe ruined the party. You handled that
really well."

We cruise across the bridge, back to our
own turf, in a way.

"Don't give me too much credit. I was kind
of scared of that guy."

"Hey, he was scary. Let's hope he's not
at the reading."

The reading?

(more)

"I'm going to read at some gallery in L.A.,"
Dad says. "This woman who owns the
place asked me. I guess she found out I
was a novelist." He shrugs. "It's not NPR,
but . . ." He glances over. "There's going
to be an open reading. Like in Venice.
Remember?"

Is he asking me to do what I think he's
asking me to do?

Two On, Two Out

Not the bottom of the ninth, though.
The game is not on the line. It's the top
of the fifth on a Wednesday evening.

I'm up. The guys are on their feet, yelling
for me. "Over the fence, Shakespeare.
Bring 'em home, baby."

I've got this pitcher figured out: slider,
fastball, curve. Slider, fastball, curve.
Like meter in a bad poem — no surprises.

I take a strike, foul one off, take a ball.
Then stroke that tepid slider into left.
It's a long single. I run hard, pull up
halfway to second, jog back, and stand
on the bag.

Mira and Dad are on their feet. He's
pointing and nodding. She says something
and they both laugh.

I like feeling my heart beat. I like sweating.
I'm well now. Totally. Like before. Maybe
better.

(more)

I'm thinking seriously about reading
when Dad reads. Like one poem. Maybe
something I wrote when I had mono.
Maybe something new.

Maybe something just for Mira.

It scares me. But in a good way.

A Poem for Poetry

I'm glad I got sick. Otherwise I might've
missed out.

I wouldn't know you like I do now. I would
have missed the way you pour down the
middle of the page like a river compared
to your pal, Prose, who takes up all
the room like a fat kid on the school bus.

People say you're hard to understand,
like you're an exchange student from Mars.
But you're not. Lots of times you say exactly
what you mean but in a different way,
one that's not so easy to forget.

You were there for me right from word
one on page one of that notebook Dad
gave me in April when I was sick. Maybe
you guided my hand, I don't know. But
finally I was able to say stuff, like about
Mom, that was kind of buried inside.
It was great to talk to her, sort of,
and for sure about her.

(more)

You were perfect for that, Poetry.
Sure, I guess I could have spilled my guts
all over the page, but you made me want
to pour things out a little more carefully.
And into prettier containers, if you know
what I mean.

Here's hoping we'll be friends for a long
time. You're very cool, you know that?

Almost as cool as baseball.